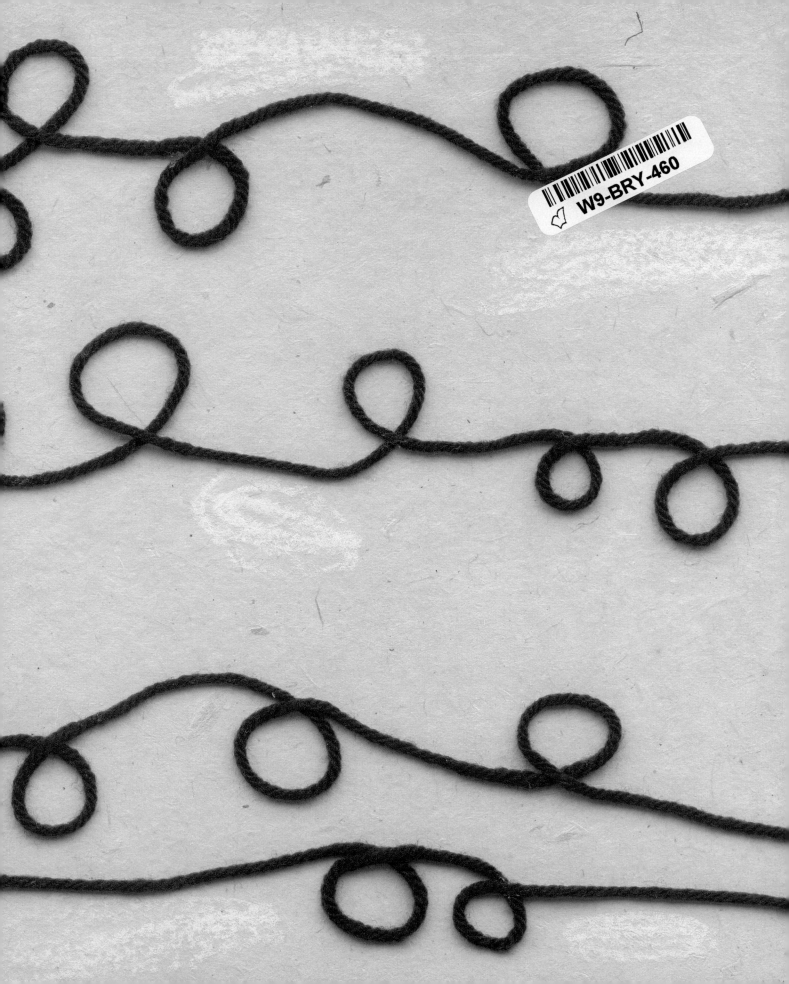

To Mary Rose Jauchen,
who is just beginning her own adventure,
and to her parents,
Mike Jauchen and Ruth Graham
D. E.

Text copyright © 2017 by David Elliott
Illustrations copyright © 2017 by Melissa Sweet

First edition 2017

Library of Congress Catalog Card Number pending
ISBN 978-0-7636-6074-1

17 18 19 20 21 22 CCP 10 9 8 7 6 5 4 3 2 1

Printed in Shenzhen, Guangdong, China

This book was typeset in Archer Medium.
The illustrations were done in watercolor, gouache, and mixed media.

Candlewick Press
99 Dover Street
Somerville, Massachusetts 02144

visit us at www.candlewick.com

Baabwaa & Wooliam

David Elliott

illustrated by Melissa Sweet

CANDLEWICK PRESS

This is Wooliam.

He is a sheep.

You will note that Wooliam is reading.

There are not many sheep who read.

But Wooliam is one of them.

This is Baabwaa, also a sheep.

In this picture, Baabwaa is knitting.

Knitting is a very practical hobby for a sheep.

It's surprising not more of them do it.

Oh well.

Baabwaa and Wooliam are best friends.

They spend most days reading and knitting.

Knitting and reading.

Sounds kind of boring.

But they like it.

One day, Wooliam looked up from his book, an adventure story. Pirates. Treasure chests. That sort of thing.

"I've been thinking," he said to Baabwaa.

"Thinking is good," Baabwaa answered. "Or so I've heard."

"We should have an adventure of our own," said Wooliam.

"Agreed!" said Baabwaa. "There are only so many sweaters one sheep can knit."

And so the two friends set off.

The day was perfect for such a thing.

The flowers were blooming.

The sun was shining.

The birds were singing.

This last bit — about the birds — was especially good because adventures usually involve some kind of trouble, and it's nice to have a little birdsong to help you through it.

There was, however, a problem.

Baabwaa and Wooliam lived in a field.

And the field was surrounded by a stone wall.

"Which way?" asked Wooliam.

"You decide," Baabwaa answered.

"Left, then," said Wooliam.

(Baabwaa thought they should have gone right.)

The two sheep walked around the field.

Once. Twice. Three times.

"Is this what adventures are like?" Baabwaa asked. "All this walking, I mean."

"I don't know," said Wooliam. "But I do know it's making me hungry."

"Me too," Baabwaa replied. "Grass, anyone?"

The two friends were just finishing their lunch
when, quite unexpectedly, they were approached
by a third sheep.

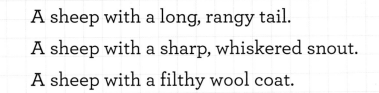

A sheep with a long, rangy tail.

A sheep with a sharp, whiskered snout.

A sheep with a filthy wool coat.

"Hey there, Muttonchops," said the . . . uh . . . sheep.
"What's shakin'?"

When he grinned, Baabwaa's heart broke.

His mother had never taught him to brush his teeth.

"We've been looking for an adventure," Wooliam said.

"Look no longer," the new sheep said. "You've found one!"

And he snapped his horrid teeth most unpleasantly.

"Run!" said Wooliam. "It's that Wolf in Sheep's Clothing I've read about."

"If this is an adventure," said Baabwaa, "I'm not a fan!"

Oddly, the birdsong did not seem to help much.

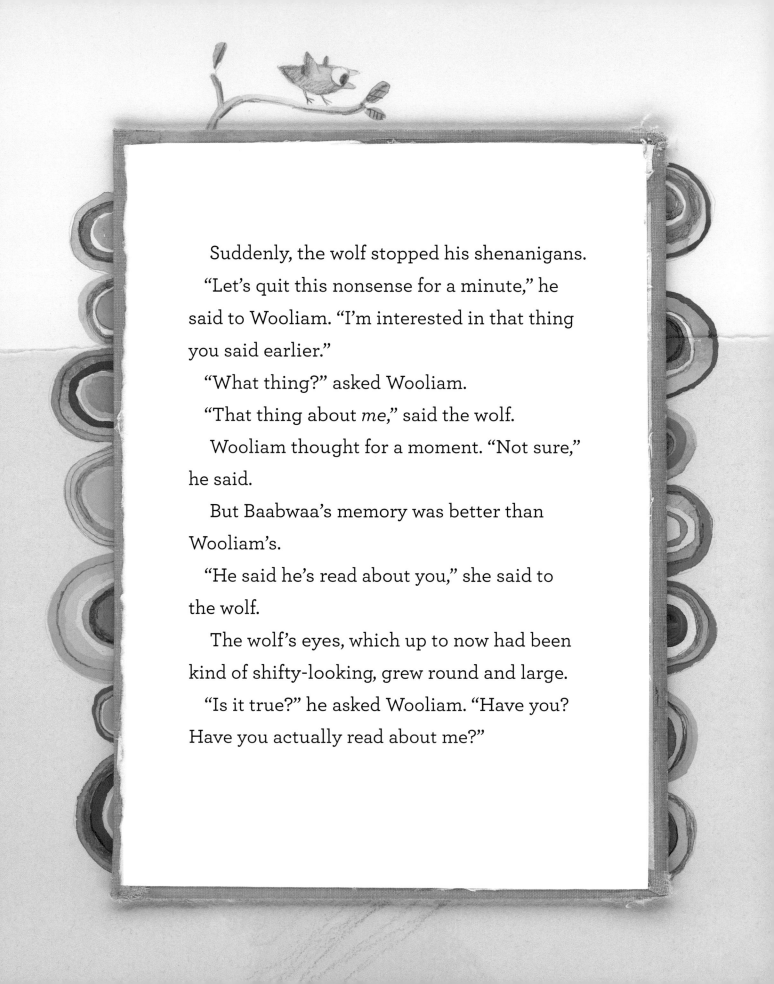

Suddenly, the wolf stopped his shenanigans.

"Let's quit this nonsense for a minute," he said to Wooliam. "I'm interested in that thing you said earlier."

"What thing?" asked Wooliam.

"That thing about *me*," said the wolf.

Wooliam thought for a moment. "Not sure," he said.

But Baabwaa's memory was better than Wooliam's.

"He said he's read about you," she said to the wolf.

The wolf's eyes, which up to now had been kind of shifty-looking, grew round and large.

"Is it true?" he asked Wooliam. "Have you? Have you actually read about me?"

"See for yourself," said Wooliam.

He reached into his backpack and pulled out a book.

The wolf took a step backward.

He looked at the blue sky. He looked at the green grass.
He looked at the big stone wall. He did not look at the book.

"Oh dear," said Wooliam. "I see the problem."

"What problem?" said the wolf. "There's no problem."

"You can't read, can you," said Wooliam.

The wolf howled a mournful lupine howl.

He dropped his shaggy lupine head.

Baabwaa's heart broke for a second time as a salty lupine tear fell on the soft ground.

"It's not my fault," the wolf cried. "I'm just not the reading kind."

"Wooliam can teach you, you know," said Baabwaa.

The wolf lifted his head and looked at Wooliam.

"Would you?" asked the wolf. "Would you do that for me?"

Wooliam didn't seem so sure.

"Of course he would," said Baabwaa. "And in the meantime, I'll knit you a new coat. That one is a disgrace."

And so Wooliam went about the business of
teaching the wolf to read.
It wasn't easy.

The wolf often jumped up in the middle of a lesson
and chased the two sheep around the field.
This irritated Wooliam no end.

"Don't let it get to you, Wooliam," said Baabwaa. "He is just
following his nature. Besides, all that reading and knitting
has taken its toll. We can use the exercise."

Eventually, after a lot of hard work and several extra help sessions, the wolf did learn to read.

And when he saw what that book had said about him, he was outraged.

"This is so unfair!" he complained. "It says here I'm cruel and sneaky!"

"And your point?" said Wooliam.

"It's not true!" the wolf insisted. "I'm just . . . rambunctious!"

"That's one word for it," said Baabwaa.

And so, over time, an unlikely
friendship formed between the wolf
and the two sheep.

One that involved a fair amount
of chasing.

But there were quiet times, too.

One afternoon when the wolf was on the second volume
of a new series he liked, and the two sheep had shed quite
a few pounds, Wooliam turned to Baabwaa. "This has been
quite an adventure, after all," he said.

Baabwaa put down her knitting, a set of snazzy leg warmers for the wolf. "I agree," she replied. "Much better than pirates."

The wolf looked up from his book.

"Can you two chattercheeks keep the noise down?" he said. "I'm reading over here."